Dear Rose and Allison,
Happy Purim!

Love
Uncle Alan
&
Aunt Darryl
3/20/00

On Purim

On Purim

BY CATHY GOLDBERG FISHMAN

ILLUSTRATED BY MELANIE W. HALL

ATHENEUM BOOKS FOR YOUNG READERS

Atheneum Books for Young Readers
An imprint of Simon & Schuster Children's Publishing Division
1230 Avenue of the Americas
New York, New York 10020

Book design by Nina Barnett.

The text of this book is set in Novarese Medium.

The illustrations are rendered in collagraph and mixed media.

Printed in Hong Kong

10 9 8 7 6 5 4 3 2 1

Library of Congress Cataloging-in-Publication Data
Fishman, Cathy.
On purim / by Cathy Goldberg Fishman; illustrated by Melanie W. Hall.
p. cm.
Summary: Uses the story of a family's preparations for the Jewish holiday of Purim
to explain the traditions connected with this celebration.
ISBN 0-689-82392-4
1. Purim—Juvenile literature. [1. Purim.] I. Hall, Melanie W., ill. II. Title.
BM695.P8F57   2000   296.4'36—dc21   98-36389

FIRST
EDITION

With love to my Purim players:
Steven, Xan, and Brittany
and to
Feivel Chanan bar Eliahu
with deep appreciation for his constant support

—C. G. F.

For the Buffoon, whose love and laughter sustains my life

—M. W. H.

"*O*h, today we'll merry, merry be," I sing as I work on my mask.

"What a happy song," my mother says. "A happy song for a happy time."

It is almost the 14th of the Hebrew month of A*dar*, and we are getting ready for the Jewish holiday of Purim. Purim is a joyous holiday when we dress up in costumes and masks. We read about Esther and how she saved the Jewish people.

I cut out holes for the eyes of my mask, and as I try to think of what else to add, I wonder, why do we wear masks on Purim?

Mordecai

King Ahasuerus

I slip my unfinished mask over my face.
"Who are you?" my father asks.
"I am Esther," I say.
My mother plops a floppy hat on Father's head.
He laughs and says, "Well, I must be your
cousin Mordecai."
My sisters and brother put on their masks, too.
My brother is King Ahasuerus. He crosses his
arms and pretends to glare at us.
"Line up," he demands. "I will choose a new
queen."
My sisters and I stay close together and giggle.

Queen Esther

"I choose you," says my brother, the king. He points at me.

"Okay, I will be queen," I say.

I do not say that Mordecai is my cousin. I do not say that I am Jewish and that my Hebrew name is Hadassah. Those are secrets the real Queen Esther kept long ago.

When Esther didn't tell the king all about herself, she was hiding who she really was. That was like wearing a mask.

Maybe that is why we wear masks on Purim, I think, as I add a veil to my mask to remind me of Purim secrets.

"Who knows the story of Purim?" my grandfather asks.

"I do!" I say.

I unroll the scroll that I made at religious school.

"Long ago in Shushan, Persia," I read, "King Ahasuerus, a silly king who partied all the time, banished his queen because she would not listen to him. He held a contest to find a new queen.

"Mordecai, a Jewish man, told his cousin, Esther, to enter the contest. He told her not to tell the king that she was Jewish because some people in Persia did not like Jews. Esther was very beautiful, and King Ahasuerus chose her to be queen.

"The king's chief advisor was an evil man named Haman."

"Boo! Boo!" my grandfather yells.

"Haman wanted everyone to bow down to him," I continue.

"Boo! Boo!" my grandfather shouts again. He shouts every time he hears Haman's name.

I keep on reading.

"Mordecai and the other Jews refused to bow down. This made Haman angry. Haman got the king's permission to kill all the Jews in Persia. He even built special gallows just to kill Mordecai.

"To stop Haman and his plan, Mordecai asked Esther to tell the king that she was Jewish and that Haman was trying to kill her and all of her people.

"There was a rule that the queen could not go to the king unless he called her. If she did, she would be killed. Even though she was afraid, Esther went to tell the king.

"After that, many plans came out differently. King Ahasuerus loved Esther so much that he listened to her. Haman was killed on the gallows meant for Mordecai, and Mordecai became the king's chief advisor. The End."

"Why were you yelling?" my brother asks Grandfather.

"Whenever we hear the name of Haman, we try to blot it out with noise," my grandfather answers.

"Boo! Boo!" my brother yells.

I think I will add jangly bells to my mask to remind me of Purim noises.

My grandmother drops spoonfuls of poppy seed and honey on small circles of pastry. My brother folds them into triangle-shaped pockets.

"I can't wait until they're baked," my sisters say.

I know why. Then we will eat the delicious cookies called *hamantashen*.

"Why are they called hamantashen?" my brother asks.

"They are the same shape as the hat Haman wore," Grandmother answers.

"Gobbling them up is another way of blotting out his name," Grandfather adds with a smile.

"Oh, today we'll merry, merry be, and *nosh* some hamantashen," I sing.

The kitchen smells like Purim as we share the first batch that comes out of the oven.

I think I will add smiling lips to my mask to remind me of Purim hamantashen.

Every Purim, my grandmother says, "Let's make *shalach manot*, gift baskets."

So we do. My sisters make baskets out of paper plates and strips of construction paper. We decorate them with sparkling sequins and curly ribbons and fill them with hamantashen, candy, and fruit.

Then we visit all our friends.

"*Chag sameach*! Happy holiday!" we say, handing them a basket as they come to the door.

I think I will add curly ribbons to my mask to remind me of Purim *shalach manot*.

"It's time for the Purim carnival," my father says on Sunday afternoon. My sisters are proud that they are old enough to work at the carnival.

I get to play the games. My favorite is Esther's Pool. I throw a fishing line behind a curtain and pretend to fish. One of my sisters puts a special prize on my line.

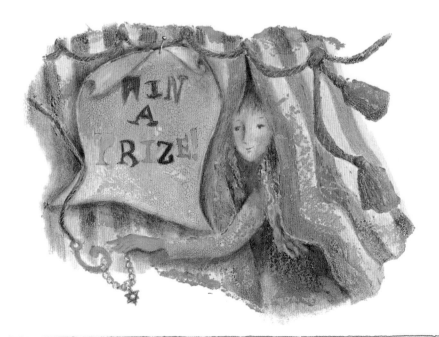

The very best part is the Purim parade. I watch
King Ahasuerus stride along, waving his scepter.
Lots of girls dance by, dressed like Queen Esther.
Haman pulls a rolling horse with Mordecai riding it.

I stand with my family and watch as the story of
Purim marches by.

I think I will finish my mask by adding red
cheeks to remind me of Purim happiness.

On the evening before the 14th of Adar, we put
on our costumes and go to synagogue. As we enter,
my father hands me some money to place in a basket.

"On Purim we remember to give *tzedakah* to the
poor," he tells me.

Everyone is in costume. I see clowns, gypsies, and lots of Purim characters. Our Rabbi is dressed like a hamantashen. Maybe we wear masks just because it's so much fun.

Everyone holds a noisemaker called a *grogger*.
We sit together and listen as our Rabbi chants the
story of Purim from a special scroll called the
Megillah. He reads in Hebrew, but I still recognize
the name of Haman.

"Boo! Boo!" I shout. The bells on my mask jangle
wildly.

We all shout, shake our groggers, and stamp our
feet. We try to blot out the name of Haman.

Purim is a strange and funny holiday.

"Where is God in the Purim story?" I ask my father.

"He is hidden in the faith of Mordecai and Esther and in their courage to do the right thing," my father says.

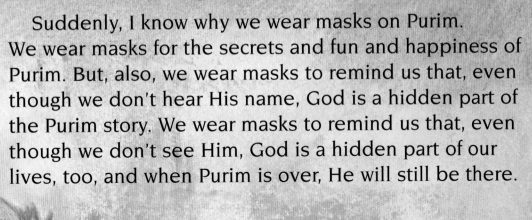

Suddenly, I know why we wear masks on Purim. We wear masks for the secrets and fun and happiness of Purim. But, also, we wear masks to remind us that, even though we don't hear His name, God is a hidden part of the Purim story. We wear masks to remind us that, even though we don't see Him, God is a hidden part of our lives, too, and when Purim is over, He will still be there.

 # GLOSSARY

Adar (ah DAR): the sixth month of the Hebrew calendar corresponding to February/March.

chag sameach (KHAHG suh MAY ahk): Hebrew for happy holiday.

Esther (EHS ter): the heroine in the Purim story.

grogger (GRAH ger): a handheld noisemaker used on Purim in the synagogue during the reading of the Megillah whenever the name of Haman is heard.

Haman (HAY mun): advisor to King Ahasuerus and the villain in the Purim story.

hamantashen (hah mun TA shen): pastries shaped like triangles and filled with honey and poppy seeds or a fruit filling. The name is a holiday pun of a German pastry called *mohn tash*, or poppy seed pocket.

King Ahasuerus (ah khas VAIR rus): the king of Persia at the time of the Purim story, usually identified as Xerxes I (486-465 B.C.E.).

Megillah (muh GIL lah): a parchment scroll with the story of Esther written on it.

Mordecai (MORE da kai): Esther's cousin and the hero of the Purim story.

nosh (nahsh): Yiddish for eat.

shalach manot (shah LAHK mah NOTE): sending gifts to friends and to the poor on Purim.

tzedakah (tseh DUH kah): money or other help given as a religious obligation to help the needy.